CHIPMUNK
IN THE
FOREST

CHIPMUNK
IN THE
FOREST

Eleanor Clymer

Drawings by Ingrid Fetz

ATHENEUM   1965   NEW YORK

CONTENTS

CHIPMUNK
IN THE
FOREST

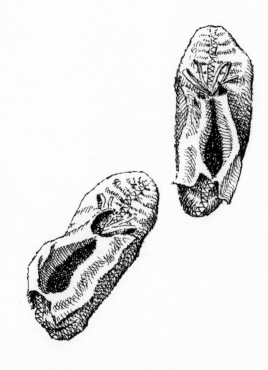

CHIPMUNK
GOES
HUNTING

LONG AGO, in the middle of a deep, dark forest, there lived an Indian boy. His name was Chipmunk.

When he was very little, his mother had called him that. She hoped he would be quick and sharp-eyed like the little animals that whisk about among the rocks and trees.

Chipmunk lived with his father and mother and his little brother in a house made of logs and bark, near a big lake.

One morning, he woke up very early. He jumped out of his bed of fur blankets and ran to the doorway to look out. He could see the other houses of the village. Smoke was going up from some of them, showing that other people were awake besides himself. His mother, Sunflower, was cooking breakfast at a fire outside the door. She smiled at him.

The sun was shining between the trees

and glittering on the lake. It would be a fine summer day.

This was a very special day, for today Chipmunk was going hunting with his uncle, Many-Deer.

Many-Deer was a chief of the village and a great hunter. He brought home plenty of deer and bear meat for his family, and many skins to make into clothes. It was an

uncle's job to teach his sister's sons to hunt;
and now Chipmunk was old enough to go
with him, to learn to track animals and to
find his way in the deep woods.

Chipmunk's father was also a skillful
hunter. His name was Flying-Arrow. He had
made the small bow and arrows and the flint-
bladed knife that Chipmunk would take with

him into the woods. Chipmunk knew it was important to learn to hunt. When he was grown-up, that was the way he would feed his family. All the boys were glad when they were big enough to hunt.

One of his friends ran past on the way to the lake.

"You're going out with your uncle to-day," he called. "You're lucky!"

Chipmunk sighed. He didn't feel lucky. For he had a secret. He was afraid—afraid of the forest.

He knew the trails close to the village, of course. He had often gone with the other boys a short way into the forest to hunt squir-rels or rabbits. But it was different in the deep woods. It was so still and dark! Who could tell what might be lurking there? Fierce animals? Ghosts? Or just endless trees among which a boy could get lost and wander for-ever?

When he sat by the fire at night and

heard the old men telling stories about the spirits that were all around, he thought of the deep woods and shivered.

Two or three times, he had been sent into the woods at night to bring back a jar of water from the brook. That was supposed to make a boy brave. But it hadn't made Chipmunk brave. Every leaf rustling or branch cracking made him tremble.

He didn't want his uncle to know about his fear. For Many-Deer was the bravest man in the village. It would be a terrible disgrace for his nephew to be afraid. So Chipmunk tried to keep his secret to himself.

Now he ate the breakfast of corn meal and maple sugar that his mother gave him. Soon he saw his uncle striding across the village from his own house, with his big bow and quiver of arrows over his shoulder, and he went inside and got his small bow and his arrows down from the wall. He made sure the bowstring was tight and the arrows sharp and straight. He put on his leather leggings and moccasins and stuck his knife in his belt.

When he came out, Many-Deer was waiting for him.

"Are you ready, Nephew?" he asked.

"I am ready," said Chipmunk, although he did not feel at all ready. To tell the truth, he was a little afraid of his uncle, too. Many-Deer was so stern and so big!

They started out, following a path between the trees that had been worn by the feet of the hunters. Many-Deer went first, and Chipmunk trotted along behind him.

It was quiet in the forest, except for the

wind in the treetops, the call of a bird, and the bubbling of a brook.

Many-Deer pointed to the brook. "This brook runs into our lake," he said. "It can help you find your way if you are lost."

"Yes, Uncle," said Chipmunk.

"See the knife-marks on the trees beside the trail," said Many-Deer. "If you see these marks, you will know that one of our hunters made them. They will help you find your way, and you can make your own marks with your knife."

"Yes, Uncle," said Chipmunk again.

They walked farther from the village, until they were in the deep woods. Here one could hardly see daylight. The trees stood in green shadows, and overhead was a roof of branches.

Chipmunk hurried to keep up with his uncle, so as not to let him out of sight.

At last they came to a clearing. The sunlight poured down through the opening in

the trees. One big tree stood alone among ferns and blueberry bushes.

"This is a good place to watch for deer," said Many-Deer. "They like to feed here. You stand behind this tree, and I will go a little way off. Keep very still."

Many-Deer moved away. His feet in their moccasins made no sound on the soft earth. Soon he was out of sight.

Chipmunk stood quietly by the tree, listening and watching. It all looked very peaceful—the branches motionless in the still air, the ferns unfolded to the sun, the patches of light between the dark hemlocks. But was anything lurking there?

Something rustled. It was only a little brown bird scratching for bugs in the dead leaves. But suddenly there was another sound. Heavy feet crunched the leaves. Something very big was coming. Chipmunk's heart pounded with fear. Was it a deer? No, it was too big for a deer. It must be a bear!

"Uncle!" he shouted. "Where are you?"

He began to run. The big creature ran, too, and now he saw that it was a great stag. It bounded away into the forest.

Many-Deer came out of his hiding place. "You frightened the stag away!" he said angrily. "Didn't I tell you to stand quietly? Why did you shout like that?"

"I thought it was a bear," said Chipmunk, feeling very much ashamed.

"A bear!" said his uncle. "I would not have let a bear come near you. You knew I

was watching close by. You have much to learn if you are going to be a hunter."

They went on into the forest, but they saw no more deer that day. At last they returned to the village.

The next morning, Many-Deer and Chipmunk started out again.

"Now remember, no running and shouting today," said Many-Deer. He went first, and Chipmunk followed along behind.

"I mustn't be afraid. I mustn't be afraid," he said to himself.

He looked up at the great trees. He could not see the sky. He could hear nothing except the wind going "sh-sh-sh" in the treetops. Suddenly a dark shadow floated over his head. It was an enormous bird with great quiet wings. It moved between the trees without a sound.

Chipmunk was so frightened that he began to run. His feet cracked the twigs and dry leaves on the ground, and the bird flew away.

Many-Deer was standing still in the path when Chipmunk ran into him. He was very angry.

"What is the matter with you, my nephew?" he asked. "I told you not to run."

"But—but that great big bird!" said Chipmunk. "It was flying over my head."

"That was an owl," said Many-Deer. "It was flying to its nest after a night's hunting. But you have scared all the game in this part of the forest. Now we will have to go to another place. See if you can behave more like

a hunter and less like a frightened rabbit."

"Yes, Uncle," said Chipmunk in a very small voice.

He followed his uncle along the trail. On and on they went, deeper into the forest. It seemed to Chipmunk that he had been walking for hours. At last he stopped for a moment to get his breath. But when he was ready to start again, he could not see his uncle. He looked for the trail, but his eyes could not pick it out. There were trees on all sides, but he saw no marks on them.

He heard the gurgling of a stream, but it seemed to be far away, somewhere below him. He looked down and saw green leaves and hemlock branches. The ground at his feet just dropped away. He was standing on the edge of a deep gorge. It was so deep that he could look out over the tops of the trees that grew there. The stream was down at the bottom.

He was all alone in this silent, mysterious

world. He was lost!

"Uncle!" he cried out. "Where are you?"

He began to run. He pushed his way between bushes. He stumbled over dead trees lying on the ground. Something snatched his foot and he fell, thinking, "I'm caught!" But it was only a root. He scrambled to his feet.

"I am here," said Many-Deer, "here in the path." Why, his voice sounded quite close! Chipmunk struggled toward it. There was the trail, only a short way back from the

gorge. Chipmunk stood before his uncle with his head down, unable to say a word.

"You are not ready to be a hunter," said Many-Deer, sternly. "Go back to the village and help your mother."

CHIPMUNK
STAYS
HOME

CHIPMUNK walked home slowly, taking care not to lose the trail again. At last he saw the village, the smoke going up from the fires, and the women working. He saw the dogs and the children playing. Everyone seemed happy and busy—everyone but himself.

His mother was startled when she saw him. "Why have you come back so soon?" she asked. "Where is your uncle? Has something happened?"

"No, nothing," said Chipmunk, in a low voice. "Uncle is hunting. He told me to come home and help you."

Sunflower understood. "So that's how it is," she said. "Very well. You may get me some water from the lake. Then you may take care of Little Brother for me."

Chipmunk did as he was told. He felt the women and children looking at him, but he did not look up.

After that, Chipmunk watched the men and other boys go out to hunt, but he stayed home. He carried water and wood for his mother. He took care of Little Brother. He knew that the people felt sorry for his parents, for it was a bad thing to have a cowardly son. If an Indian boy did not become a good hunter, his family and the whole village would suffer.

The other boys made fun of Chipmunk. "You have an easy life," they said. "You are doing girls' work."

But it was not so easy to take care of Little Brother. He was a mischievous little boy. He liked to upset the water jar. He liked to hide Chipmunk's things, to tease him. And he thought it was fun to hide himself, so that Chipmunk had to look for him.

Chipmunk would search behind trees, under piles of leaves, in the other houses of the village. Little Brother would laugh when he was found. He thought it was a fine game.

One day he took Chipmunk's bow and arrows. "I am going hunting," he said. And

he ran off down the path into the forest. Chipmunk had to run fast to catch him.

Another day he ran down to the lake. Chipmunk found his footprints in the sand and thought Little Brother had fallen into the water and drowned. At last he found him hiding under a canoe.

"That was a good joke," said Little Brother.

Chipmunk did not think it was such a good joke, but he tried to be patient. After all, his brother was very little. Someday he would have more sense.

Sometimes Chipmunk's mother and father talked quietly about their sons as they sat before the fire.

"It would be a good thing if our older son had the courage of his little brother," said Flying-Arrow, sadly.

"Chipmunk is a good boy," Sunflower would say. "Don't be impatient. One day he will lose his fear."

"I hope you are right," Flying-Arrow would answer.

The summer passed, and winter came. Snow covered the ground. Every day the hunters went out to look for game. At first there was plenty. But it was a long, cold winter. Little by little, the deer disappeared. The bears were sleeping in their caves. The squirrels stayed in their hollow trees. The hungry wolves ran through the woods at night, looking for food.

Chipmunk, waking up in his warm bed, heard them howling and shivered. He looked sleepily at the glowing fire in the middle of the floor and thought of the cold, lonely woods out beyond the village. It was good

to be safe and warm.

One morning, Many-Deer and Flying-Arrow started out together. They were going to hunt on the other side of the lake. Perhaps there they would have better luck.

Sunflower put a little food into a pouch for them. Chipmunk watched them go. He felt the cold wind that blew in when Flying-Arrow lifted the bearskin at the door. He thought how brave the men were and felt sorry that he was not of more use to them. He almost wished they would take him along, but he knew he would only be in the way. He went out and brought in some firewood.

On the bed, Little Brother was playing with a tiny bow that his father had made for him.

"Someday I am going to be a great hunter," he boasted. "I'll bring home so much meat that we will have enough for the whole village."

"Don't brag, little one," said Chipmunk. "It is better to boast *after* you have brought home the meat."

Little Brother thought about this. He was quiet for a while. Then he said, "All right, I will bring home the meat first. Then you will see."

And he pretended to shoot an arrow at the roof.

Chipmunk ran out, broke the ice at the edge of the lake, and filled a jar with water. It was bitter cold, and the wind whistled over the frozen water. He hurried back to the house and sat down to scrape rabbit skins, which his mother would use to make a blanket.

Suddenly he looked around. It was very quiet all of a sudden. Where was Little Brother? He was not in the house.

"Where has he gone?" he asked.

Sunflower had been grinding corn meal. She was so busy that she had not seen Little Brother go.

"Perhaps he is next door playing with his friend Little Beaver," she said.

Chipmunk ran to Little Beaver's house, but his brother was not there. Nobody had seen him.

Chipmunk could not understand it. He ran home and looked under all the blankets. Surely Little Brother would not play tricks out of doors in such cold weather as this! He ran out again.

"Have you seen my little brother?" he shouted to some boys who were playing on the ice.

"Yes," one of them answered. "He went off to the forest."

Chipmunk thought they were teasing him, but he ran to the edge of the forest. Sure enough, there were small footprints in the snow.

Then he remembered what he had said that morning: "It is better to boast *after* you have brought home the meat."

And Little Brother had answered that he would bring home the meat. Perhaps he had really gone hunting!

THE
SEARCH

WHAT SHOULD Chipmunk do now? Should he call someone? The men were all away hunting. And how could he tell his mother that he had not watched Little Brother? Should he tell the other boys? They would laugh at him. They would say, "Your little brother has more courage than you."

No, he would have to go himself.

Chipmunk ran back to the house. He put on his leggings and his warm shirt. He took his flint knife and started out.

The little footprints led him along the path into the forest. There everything was cold and still. The trees stood like unfriendly giants in the white snow. The snow lay on their branches like the white hair of old, old men.

Chipmunk could hear his heart beating. He could see his breath in the cold air, and he shivered as he peered between the trees. What lay there, deep in the forest? What wild animals were waiting for him? He thought of that great bird he had seen once. Even if it was only an owl, it was frightening because it was so quiet.

He heard a branch crack. Was something coming after him? No, it had cracked from the cold.

But it would not do to stand still. He had to hurry. The footprints were not easy to see on the beaten path, but here and there Little Brother had strayed off the path, and in the soft snow his tracks were plain.

Here was a place where he had sat down, or perhaps fallen down.

"Shall I call him?" Chipmunk wondered. He did not like to shout, alone in the quiet woods. What if a wolf or a bear should hear him? But he had to call.

"Oh-hoh! Little Bro-ther! Where are you?"

"Where are you," a voice answered. It was only an echo.

He went on. Now the prints left the path. There were rabbit tracks, and the little

moccasin prints followed them. Chipmunk stepped off the path, too. He did not like to leave the path, but he thought he could find it again by following his own footprints.

But snowflakes were beginning to fall. Slowly they drifted down. They would cover the tracks, and how would he find the path again? Chipmunk looked around wildly. He would never remember the way he had come unless he marked the trail. He pulled out his knife and cut into the bark of a tree. He made another cut farther on. He broke off branches here and there. With luck, he would find his way back.

"Oh-hoh!" he called again. "Little *Bro-ther*! Where *are* you?"

He heard a creaking noise. But it was only two branches rubbing together in the wind.

Chipmunk felt angry at Little Brother for making all this trouble for him. He would have liked to turn around and go home to the warm house, the glowing fire. But how could he? Could he sit by the fire, while Little Brother was out here in the snow? No, he could not.

He went on, keeping his eye on the little footprints. But now the snow fell faster, and the footprints began to disappear. He hurried, still breaking off branches and making marks with his knife, though his hands were so cold that he could hardly hold it.

Suddenly he heard a loud squeak. He spun around and saw a gray animal among the bushes. Was it a wolf coming for him? No, it was only a fox that had caught a mouse; it was the mouse that had squeaked. Maybe this was a good sign. The fox had had luck in hunting, and maybe he, too, would be lucky and find his brother.

But what if he were not? What if he had to stay in the woods all night? He could climb a tree, but there were wildcats in the woods, and they could climb trees, too. It was better

not to think about it.

He called again, and this time he thought
he heard an answer. He stumbled on, wiping
the snow from his eyes and hair.

"Little Brother! Where are you?" he
shouted.

This time he did hear an answer. A little
voice called, "I'm here! Come and help me!"

Chipmunk hurried toward the sound.

"Here I am!" he shouted. "Come here!
Come to me!"

"I can't come," Little Brother called. "I can't climb up! Come down and help me!"

"Where are you?" Chipmunk called angrily. "I can't see you. This is no time to play hide-and-seek."

"I'm not playing," said Little Brother. "I'm down here! I can't get out!"

His voice sounded frightened, and very faint and far away. "Come down," he had said. But where was he?

Chipmunk looked around, and suddenly he knew. The white ground fell away at his feet. He was standing at the edge of the gorge, and Little Brother was at the bottom. When Chipmunk peered down between the trees, he could see a small figure waving up at him.

"How did you get there?" he shouted.

"I was running after a rabbit," Little

Brother shouted back, "and I fell down. Come and get me. Hurry up! I'm so cold!"

Chipmunk wondered how he was going to get Little Brother out of there. If he went down, he might not be able to get up again, and they would both be trapped; for he did not know how long the gorge was, or whether there was any other way out of it. But he had to try, and quickly. It was afternoon now, and the short winter day would soon be over.

He took a deep breath and started down. At first he managed to stay on his feet, catching at tree trunks as he went down the steep slope. But there was ice under the drifted snow, and his feet slipped. At last he just sat down and slid to the bottom.

Little Brother ran to him. "Oh, I'm so glad you came!" he chattered. "I tried to climb out, but I couldn't. I thought I'd have to stay here forever!"

He wanted to tell all about it, but Chipmunk had no time to listen. He felt the little
boy all over to be sure he had not broken any
bones. No, he was not hurt. He had rolled
down in the soft snow, and by some good
fortune had not hit any trees. But he was very
cold. They must get home as fast as possible.

THE
FOREST
IS
HOME

"WE MUST CLIMB UP," said Chipmunk.

"I can't move," said Little Brother. "My feet have no feeling."

Chipmunk wished he could make a fire. But he had no fire-making tools, and even if he had had some, there would have been no time.

"Sit down and I will rub your feet," he said. He rubbed as hard as he could, until some warmth came back to them.

"Now come," he said. "It will soon be dark."

He started to climb, pulling the little boy by the hand. But Little Brother stumbled and fell flat in the snow. Chipmunk tried to push him up the slope, bracing himself against a tree. They struggled a little way up and then fell back.

Chipmunk picked himself up and stood still, catching his breath. The snow sifted lazily down. Blue shadows of twilight lay between the trees. Chipmunk wondered how he and Little Brother would ever get home. By the time he managed to get his brother up to the top of the gorge, it would be dark. Then how would he find the knife-marks he had made? Somewhere nearby was the hunters' trail, but he had no hope of finding that either.

Little Brother looked up at him, waiting. The trees seemed to be waiting, too. They were like black giants, with snow on their

heads. In the silence, Chipmunk heard something.

It was a tinkling sound, like water running. It seemed to come from somewhere below. He turned and went back to the bottom of the gorge.

Now he heard the sound more clearly. It was water running. Suddenly he remembered! A stream ran at the bottom of the gorge. He began to dig. Yes, there it was, under the snow.

He remembered his uncle's words: "If you follow the brook, it will lead you to our lake."

Was this the same brook? Perhaps not, but maybe it would also lead to the lake. If they followed it, maybe they would get out.

"Come," he said, taking Little Brother's hand. "I think I know the way home."

They pushed their way between bushes and over rocks, following the stream. Sometimes it was hidden by drifts. Sometimes the water flowed, black and shiny, between snow-covered boulders. Once or twice their feet slipped into icy water, but they went on.

At last the ground levelled off. Chipmunk sighed with relief. They were out of the gorge. The stream curved to meet a brook that ran into it.

Chipmunk looked around. He knew that brook. He saw trail marks on the trees.

"Now I know the way," he said. "Here is the path."

Now they could see the sky and some bright stars. The snow had stopped falling and the sun had set; but it was not altogether dark. The white snow reflected the stars and gave enough light to see by.

"We'll be home soon," said Chipmunk.

"I can't walk any more," said Little Brother. "I'm too tired."

"But we can't stop now," said Chipmunk.

"I just want to sit down," said Little Brother.

"Well, I'll carry you," said Chipmunk, and he took the little boy on his back. He stumbled along until he thought he could not walk another step. Little Brother was certainly heavy.

"You must get down now," he said. But there was no answer. Little Brother was asleep. Chipmunk would have to go on. It couldn't be much farther.

But suddenly he heard shouts. Men were coming toward them. Some had torches

made of burning branches in their hands. What was happening? Were they looking for someone?

"Oh-hoh!" they shouted. "Chipmunk! Where are you?"

Why, they were looking for *him*!

"Here I am!" he shouted back, trying to go faster.

There was his father! There was his uncle, and the other men from the village.

"Where have you been?" Flying-Arrow demanded angrily. "Where is your brother?"

"Here I am," said Little Brother, waking up and sliding to the ground.

"What kind of game is this?" Many-Deer asked. "We thought you were lost. What is the matter with you? Why are you in the forest at night?"

Chipmunk looked at his father and his uncle and could not say a word. He had made them angry again.

But Little Brother could talk fast enough.

"I was lost," he said. "I ran away to the woods. I wanted to go hunting, but I fell down a big hill. My brother found me."

"Is this true?" Flying-Arrow asked.

"Yes," said Chipmunk. "It was my fault. I should have watched him more carefully. I am sorry, Father, if you are angry."

But Flying-Arrow did not look angry any more. He had only been angry because he was frightened. He was afraid that both his sons were lost; and when he saw them safe, he scolded them as all parents would do.

Now he asked, "But were you not afraid of the forest?"

"Yes, I was," said Chipmunk in a low voice. He did not want to admit that he had thought of going home by himself.

"Weren't you afraid of getting lost?" Many-Deer asked.

"Yes, but I remembered what you told me," said Chipmunk. "I watched for signs on the trees, and I made my own signs."

Then he remembered the gorge. "And then," he went on, "I found the stream. We followed it back to the trail. Then Little Brother could not walk any more, so I carried him."

Flying-Arrow nodded. "You have done well," he said. "You are a good boy. Come, we must go home. Your mother is waiting." He picked up the little boy in one arm. Then, with his hand on his older son's shoulder, he started for home.

Sunflower was waiting at the door. She
put her hand on Chipmunk's head and looked
at him lovingly. She did not weep or cry out,
but he could see how glad she was to have
him home safe. She took Little Brother in her
arms and put him to bed. He was so tired that
he did not even wake up.

That night there was a celebration. The hunters had brought home a great stag, enough for the whole village. As many as could get in gathered in the house of Many-Deer. The fire glowed, and they all ate until they could eat no more.

After the feast, Many-Deer began to talk. "This is a happy day," he said. "My sister's son will be a great hunter. He may even be a chief someday, after I am gone. He went into the forest and found his way alone. His brother was lost, and he found him."

Chipmunk was amazed. He had not thought his uncle was pleased with him or would praise him before the whole village. He sat on the floor behind his mother and tried to hide.

"Stand up, Nephew, so that we can see you," said Many-Deer. "Tell us how you found your brother."

Chipmunk told his story. But he did not

feel like boasting. "I was really afraid," he said. "I heard the big animals moving in the forest."

"You did not come home without your brother," said Many-Deer. "You remembered what you had learned. You made your own trail-marks. Perhaps they will help others find their way in the woods. You were

afraid, but you went ahead just the same. No man can do more than that."

He smiled at his nephew.

"Tomorrow we will go hunting together," he said. "Soon you will shoot your first deer."

After that everyone went home. Chipmunk and his mother and father went back to their own house and lay down to sleep.

But Chipmunk could not sleep. He crept to the doorway and pushed aside the bearskin. He looked out at the forest. The trees stood like friendly giants in the snow. The moon shone down with a white, glittering light. An owl flew silently by, like a great feathery shadow.

Chipmunk felt happy. He loved the forest. It was his home.